Dear Liar

A Biography in Two Acts

by Jerome Kilty

Adapted from the correspondence between
Bernard Shaw
and
Mrs. Patrick Campbell

A SAMUEL FRENCH ACTING EDITION

SAMUEL FRENCH

FOUNDED 1830

New York Hollywood London Toronto

SAMUELFRENCH.COM

ISBN   978-0-573-60783-7   Printed in U.S.A.   #6040

MUSIC USE NOTE

Licensees are solely responsible for obtaining formal written permission from copyright owners to use copyrighted music in the performance of this play and are strongly cautioned to do so. If no such permission is obtained by the licensee, then the licensee must use only original music that the licensee owns and controls. Licensees are solely responsible and liable for all music clearances and shall indemnify the copyright owners of the play and their licensing agent, Samuel French, Inc., against any costs, expenses, losses and liabilities arising from the use of music by licensees.

IMPORTANT BILLING AND CREDIT
REQUIREMENTS

All producers of *DEAR LIAR must* give credit to the Author of the Play in all programs distributed in connection with performances of the Play, and in all instances in which the title of the Play appears for the purposes of advertising, publicizing or otherwise exploiting the Play and/or a production. The name of the Author *must* appear on a separate line on which no other name appears, immediately following the title and *must* appear in size of type not less than fifty percent of the size of the title type.

NOTE ON THE PLAY

There are only two characters: the actor who speaks the words of G.B.S. and the actress who speaks those of Mrs. Patrick Campbell. He is dressed in a dark, semi-formal suit or perhaps a smoking jacket, whatever seems best for the particular actor playing the role. She should have three lovely evening dresses that are at once "modern" and "period." Again, they should be designed to show the actress off as beautifully as possible. No attempt should be made to represent the features of either Shaw or Mrs. Campbell. A touch of Irish accent, in English-speaking countries, should be used by Shaw. She will wear one dress in the First Act, one in the first part of the Second, and another after she returns to the Stage for the last part of the Play. The last dress should be the simplest of all and should be designed to help the actress feel older than she was at the beginning.

The set is very simple: a semi-circular arrangement of drapes. A lovely writing desk for her with a feminine and charming small armchair before it. A small footstool is under the desk. He will have a standing desk with an appropriate high stool in front of it and, Down Right of the desk, a small chair or hassock which can be easily carried about. In the middle of the Stage is a practical hatbox with a hinged top standing on a small, light table. There should be an entrance Up Center. Behind her desk, Stage Left, there is a break in the drapes to suggest a window. The desks are placed to face diagonally out-wards.

ACT I: covers the period 1899 to 1914.

ACT II: from 1914 to 1939.

Dear Liar

ACT ONE

TIME: *1899–1914.*

AT RISE: THE ACTOR *and* ACTRESS *enter and walk to either side of the hatbox.*

ACTRESS. (*To the audience.*) Good evening.

ACTOR. Good evening.

ACTRESS. For forty years of their very public lives there existed a private and infinitely intriguing relationship between the famous English actress, Mrs. Patrick Campbell, and George Bernard Shaw. The well-known vegetarian—

ACTOR. *And* playwright.

ACTRESS. And playwright. When Mr. Shaw was, as he said himself, old enough to know better, he fell head over heels in love with Mrs. Campbell. He dreamed he walked on air; he ran singing through the streets to meet her, his Stella Stellarum, his glorious white marble lady. His love, he said, was everlasting and undying—

ACTOR. (*To audience.*) But forty years later, when he heard of her death, Shaw wrote, "Everyone is greatly relieved; herself, I should think, most of all, for she could not live with real people in the real world. Still she was a great enchantress, and she enchanted me, amongst the rest." (*The* ACTRESS *opens the lid of the hatbox.*) This is the story of that enchantment told in their own words in the hundreds of letters they sent to one another over the years, letters which they both saved, fought over; returned to each other and very nearly lost in the second world war.

ACTRESS. (*To audience. As she speaks, the* ACTOR *takes*

5

out one packet of letters and looks through them.) In 1940 "Mrs. Pat," as she was known to the public, died in the South of France. With her were all the letters she kept in this hatbox, under her bed. The English lady who buried her left everything else behind and managed to get the hatbox over to England just five days before the Germans were in Paris.

ACTOR. (*To audience. The* ACTRESS *now takes out the other packet of letters from the hatbox.*) But it is forty years earlier that our play begins. Imagine, if you will, the end of the last century. Victoria is still on the throne; England, the most modern of modern nations; the world wars are still to come.

ACTRESS. Mrs. Patrick Campbell is at the height of her career. With Ellen Terry she had reigned over the English theatre for nearly ten years. She had already created many of her most famous roles but her *most* famous, Eliza Doolittle, was yet to come.

ACTOR. I—for we speak now in the words of George Bernard Shaw— (*He hands packet of letters to her.*)

ACTRESS. And Mrs. Patrick Campbell— (*She hands her packet to him.*)

SHAW. I was ending my first career as music and drama critic and was beginning to turn out plays of my own— none of them achieving much success at first. Inspired by the beauty and artistry of Mrs. Campbell in The Second Mrs. Tanqueray, I started work on a new play, Caesar And Cleopatra, hoping that she might act in it when it was finished. With this in mind I invited her down to my cottage in Hindhead for a weekend visit.

CAMPBELL. But it is all here, in the letters. Will you begin please, Mr. Shaw?

SHAW. With pleasure, Mrs. Campbell— (*They make a formal bow and then cross to their desks. As* SHAW *recites his first letter,* CAMPBELL *begins by holding a single letter as if she is just reading it.*)
Blen Cathra Hindhead, 12th of April, 1899.
Dear Mrs. Patrick Campbell:

We have this house until the 14th May only; so come quickly. Mrs. Shaw will be delighted to see you.

The vegetables have triumphed over their traducers. I was told that my meatless diet was so poor that I could not repair the bones that were broken in my foot. So I have just had an X-radiograph taken and lo! perfectly mended bone so beautifully white that I have left instructions that, if I die, a glove stretcher is to be made out of them and sent to you as a souvenir.

(MRS. CAMPBELL *laughs; puts letter down, sits and listens.*)

I have seen your latest photograph. Wonderful as it is, I would have photographed you in bed, saying, "It's tempting Providence." After all, there are lots of beautiful people about, but they can't all take a filament of grey matter from their brains and thread it through the hole in the dramatist's needle. It is your power to do that that is the real gift . . . I do hope you can come . . . Yours sincerely, (*Pantomimes signature.*) George Bernard Shaw.

(SHAW *reads from a single letter as she speaks. This is only to establish the convention: it is not repeated again.*)

CAMPBELL.
33 Kensington Sq. W., 21 April, 1899.
My dear Mr. Shaw:

I dread seeing my photographs—the days of dewlaps have arrived! God help me and all women! I am afraid I won't be able to accept your invitation. Oh that I had mislaid countless sons and daughters and that they would all turn up today or tomorrow and prevent me accepting an offer to tour in America—20 weeks at so many dollars a minute!

I've been asked to appear in Rostand's wonderful fairy play. Wouldn't it be nice if you "Englished" it for us? Do let me know.

May God bless you for the smiles you make us smile and forgive you for those literary lack-of-taste misdemeanors that make us squirm.

>Yours sincerely, Beatrice Stella Campbell.

SHAW.

Dear Mrs. Patrick Campbell:

I don't think it would do for me to meddle with Rostand's fairy scheme; it would give it a flavour of brimstone at once. Give your contemporaries a chance. Turn to the rising suns: I am exhausted, hackneyed, vulgarized, and far too old for these games: 45 last July as ever was . . .

>(*During this he carries hatbox and stand* U. C. *where it remains.*)

>Yours sincerely, G. Bernard Shaw.

CAMPBELL. (*To audience.*) In the fifth month of the new century my husband was killed in the fighting in South Africa. We had been married for 16 years and the loneliness was overwhelming. The only thing was to plunge back into my work and within a year I had opened in a new play.

SHAW.

7th November, 1901.

My dear Mrs. Patrick Campbell:

I finally secured a seat to your performance. It was really a great achievement and the use of Handel's music was a fine touch. I do, however, think the Hallelujah Chorus might be improved by steeping in boiling water for ten minutes or so. Oh, yes! It is not natural that your leading man should die unassisted the way he does, especially after gurgling like Othello with his throat cut.

However, all that is nothing. The impression was overwhelming.

>Yours enthusiastically, Bernard Shaw.

CAMPBELL. (*To audience.*) After this I appeared in a series of wonderful plays, one success after another; Pelleas and Melisande, Hedda Gabler and Bella Donna, which I took back and forth between England and America. It was some years before I heard from Mr. Shaw again. My children were growing up and already getting married; my son, Beo, in 1909 and my daughter, Stella, in 1911.

SHAW. (*To audience.*) And I was turning out one play after another. *Fanny's First Play* was a walloping success running for nearly 600 performances and began to bring in money such as I'd never seen before. And after this had opened, I set to work in earnest on a play I'd long planned for Mrs. Campbell—*Pygmalion*—and early in 1911 it was finished. I went to her house to read it to her and, after she'd heard it, the next day she wrote—

CAMPBELL.

My dear Mr. Shaw:

What a play. I must confess I was surprised to hear those unpleasant sounds of Eliza's cockney accent coming out of your mouth. But if you're really in earnest the next step is to tell me what the business proposal is— when, where and with whom and *perhaps* one day I will . . .

(*She rises and speaks quickly to audience.*) And he arrived for tea on a glorious June afternoon with laughter in his eyes and a contract in his pocket. When he went away, I had the strange impression that our friendship was ripening perhaps *too* rapidly; when I received his next note I was certain of it. I caught him in the act of slipping it under the door.

SHAW. (*He walks toward her and pantomimes putting note under the door.*) You knew it would happen! I went calmly to your house to discuss business with you, as hard as nails, and as I am a living man, I fell head over heels in love with you in the first thirty seconds. How long did it last? For thirty hours! Why, I dreamed and walked on air all the following afternoon just as if my next birthday were my twentieth. (*He returns to his desk.*)

CAMPBELL. But you are not twenty and the theatre is business . . . a very big business! If, I tell you, "if,"

I can get the right people together to do it I will be your pretty slut. That far I will go.

SHAW. Very well, then, to business: I am going to break the shattering news that you have captured me . . . for your own theatre! You see! That is the worst of having anything to do with me: you are dragged at once into the brazen atmosphere behind which my poor timid little soul hides and cowers and dreams. (CAMPBELL *crosses up to "window."*) Your plans will be known to everyone before this letter reaches you, with a romantic glamor round them, but still sufficiently correct to make it necessary for you to play with your cards on the table. So beware!

CAMPBELL. I *always* play with my cards on the table, not in my pocket. *That* was your game. All that pretense of "being in the neighborhood."

SHAW. A perfectly respectable ruse. What's the matter? Are you afraid you might involve your heart with this blarneying Irish liar and actor . . . as he has with you? Or are you afraid you won't?

CAMPBELL. (*During* SHAW's *speech she has slowly crossed to his desk and now is speaking directly into his eyes.*) Beatrice Webb is right, you are a sprite. And how can one fall in love with a sprite? "Will you come on Friday and I promise we can be *alone!*" (*She returns to her area.*)

SHAW. (*To audience.*) If Stella wanted to capture you you might as well go willingly, for she was irresistible. All of London knew her charms from across the footlights but I was learning them from a much different perspective. I would not have believed I had that left in me. (*To* CAMPBELL.)

Dear Stella:

Many thanks for Friday; and for a Saturday of delightful dreams back up in the clouds. I am all right now, though, down on earth again with all my cymbals and side drums and "blaring vulgarities" in full blast; but it would be meanly cowardly to pretend that you are not a very wonderful lady, or that the spell did not work most enchantingly on me for fully twelve hours . . . G.B.S.

CAMPBELL. Shall we keep to business, Mr. Shaw? . . . I have made a formal offer for the theatre and have let the world know that I am going into management and that I may act in Mr. Shaw's Eliza. Perhaps you have already seen it in the papers. Who will play the part opposite to me of—of—who is it?

SHAW. Henry Higgins!

CAMPBELL. Yes, Henry Higgins, I don't know yet, but never mind. We will find someone. For—Higgins.

SHAW. We cannot have "someone" to play Higgins. It's just as important a part as Eliza. Stella, beware! If you attempt management on the one-star system, nothing, not even my genius added to your own, can save you from final defeat. "Male and female created He them." Your public is more than half feminine. You cannot satisfy their longing for a male to idealize. And how could they idealize a poor salaried supporting actor, pushed into a corner and played off the stage? Do you want to be Eleanora Duse: a hammer without an anvil? Yes, produce Pygmalion with a cheap Higgins and I'll tell you exactly what will happen. You will have an uproarious personal success; but the house will be under two hundred pounds. At the end of a few weeks business will stagger. You will be terrified and will spend wildly on advertisements. You will drop to one hundred and twenty pounds. You will struggle on until you have lost every farthing and then it will be America, with all its horrors, to recoup yourself! No, Stella, no no no. I must have a heroic Higgins, not just "anyone" and I will not let you ruin me nor yourself. I could not love thee, dear, so much loved I not money more. (*Obstinately turns his back to her.*)

CAMPBELL. Oh, Mr. Shaw, you're such a clown! I think I'll call you "Joey"—"Joey the Clown." One knows only too well that a two star show is better than a one star and that an all star show is fit only for Kings and Queens.

SHAW. If you know that why are you being so difficult?

CAMPBELL. I'm not being difficult. If you don't care if I'm happy in my work, there are many that do. James Barrie has a new play for me and Chas. Frohman offers me a fortune to take it to America!

SHAW. Yes, yes, I know all about that but for the love of God, Stella, you must be reasonable.

CAMPBELL. I feel thoroughly unreasonable and uncomfortable haggling with you this way. If Higgins is a more important part than Eliza then get a male star and some "little actress" and I'll step out.

SHAW. Stella, talk sense! You an established star, a veteran, in fact, must have an established star to play opposite you.

CAMPBELL. A veteran! How dare you! I'm not a veteran! Veteran! That makes me feel like the horse that once won the Derby and has been put out to pasture ever since. A veteran! One would think that my hair's a wig, my eyes are glass and my legs wooden. Well, I've got my eyes, my hair's my own and my legs are as good as the best. And I *won't* be a day over thirty-nine! Of course, I do have a daughter who's twenty-eight, but what of that? It happens in India all the time.

SHAW. Have you finished?

CAMPBELL. No I have not. I was told today that you only wanted me to play Eliza for the joy of making a fool of me, so everyone can say "the joke, the enormous joke" of my playing a girl! Well we'll see who has the last laugh. I wonder what your nonsensical play would be without me!

SHAW. But I want my Liza and no other Liza. I wrote the play to have my Liza. And I must have a proper Higgins *for* my Liza.

CAMPBELL. Then you listen to reason.

SHAW. I won't listen to reason! I'll sit here and howl. I can howl for twenty years, getting louder and louder all the time. All I ask is to have my own way in everything! (*He folds his arms.*)

CAMPBELL. Oh, darling!

SHAW. Mr. Shaw! If you please.

CAMPBELL. (*Mocking and tender.*) I call you "darling" because "dear Mr. Shaw" means nothing at all—whilst darling means most dear and most dear means a man, and a mind and a speaking—such as you and your mind and your speech! I long to get on with the whole thing and call rehearsals on Sept. 1st.

SHAW. September 1st is agreeable to me if we find the right Higgins. I will not budge from this position. (*He laughs and looks at her.*) Our friends are beginning to talk about us. Cartloads of chaff are falling on me like snow on Mont Blanc. Mrs. Shaw and I were with James Barrie on Monday night. At eleven I rose to go. Barrie said in his slowest Scotch manner, "Shall ye be seeing Mrs. Campbell again tonight?" Such is the ribaldry I have brought on you. (*To audience.*) I wish I could fall in love without telling everybody. I shall be fifty-six on the twenty-sixth of this month, and I have not yet grown up. I must go now and read this letter to my wife, Charlotte. My love affairs are her unfailing amusement. (*Rises and crosses up to desk.*) Oh, forgive this blasphemy; but my head is still bad and it makes me naughty—Stella— (*She doesn't reply.*) Stella! September 1st—yes?

CAMPBELL. (*After a moment of resistance.*) September first—yes.

SHAW. (*To audience.*) But it was not to be, not yet. A few weeks later, shortly after I'd begun my annual holiday on the Continent, Stella was involved in a horrible taxicab accident; (CAMPBELL *pulls footstool from under desk and puts feet on it.*) which brought our plans to a crashing halt and kept her from acting for more than a year. She was driving to the Albert Hall, holding on her lap her ever-present pekingese, this one named *Pinky Panky Poo.* (SHAW *sits on high stool.*)

(*During the ensuing section, while* CAMPBELL *is ill, the two* ACTORS *do not look at each other as they speak.*

SHAW *talks to the* S. L. *part of the house; she, to the* S. R. *part.*)

CAMPBELL. It was a blinding bang!—my head rose six inches and then the hemorrhage came down my face under the skin, and I have been a sight of sights ever since with aches and pains in every inch of me and bruises as large as saucers—I'm afraid I can't play Bella Donna again—it must close— Nor Liza now, I fear. May Strachey begged me to write and say it would be grand and that you rather owed it to me—to let us have Liza to take with us on the rest cure in France. I can read to her—what the world will never hear now and we would let no other soul see it.—Write and make me get well. A letter a day won't be enough.

SHAW. Not one but a thousand letters will I write to you. What a close call that was! Thank God, you're not dead. A rest cure is the only thing. I am on holiday here in the Bavarian Alps but I will send you a rough proof of *Pygmalion* to take with you. I warn you beforehand, however, that if you read it again you are lost; you will be at my feet at once with your dark hair looking dyed because of the gleaming of my brown shoes through the roots. Is it Lady Strachey you are with? If it is, what will she think of me when you trail your victim before her? I solemnly protest that when I went into your house in Kensington Square I was a man of iron, insolently confident in my own impenetrability. And in thirty seconds—oh, Stella, if you had a rag of decency it *couldn't* have happened. Is this dignified? Is it sensible? At my age—a driveller—a dotard! I will conquer this weakness, or better still, trade in it and write plays about it.

CAMPBELL. Write plays about whatever you wish but not, please, about us! . . . My daughter, Stella, when she was little, used to sing a song which she thought was funny. It began like this:

> He's mad, mad, mad,
> He's clean gone off his nut

He cleans his boots with strawberry jam
He eats his hat whenever he can
He's mad—
It's really about you. (*She suddenly moves her head too quickly, giving it a painful twinge.*) I still have two black eyes and some screw-like pains in my shoulder.

SHAW. Your mention of Stellinetta reminds me of a time I puzzled her with a piece of Irish folly. We were sitting in the front box at the Savoy at some idiotic performance of *Arms and the Man;* and the audience gave me a sort of ovation at the end. My impulse was to rise and bless them— (*He makes an elaborate cross in the air.*) it's true, I often feel like the Pope. She thought I was cracked, poor infant!

CAMPBELL. You seem to be having a merry time. I wish I were with you but they won't even let me sit up for more than an hour at a stretch. Not to speak of motoring! . . . Here at Aix I am looking at a glorious world, when I look up—and out—but the scullery maids in their pearls and fashions with their bloody nails and sealing-wax lips make my hair stand on end—I have never been to a fashionable cure place before—I am a little astounded.—"Laugh and the world laughs with you, snore and you sleep alone." Perhaps some day, if you are very good and behave properly at rehearsal I will write you a love letter.

SHAW. A love letter! *Sancta simplicitas!* When did you ever write me anything else? No; let me write; and do you *pray* for us both; for there is always danger when that devilment Love is at work! Ah! I wish you were with me, you'd keep me out of pickles such as I got into yesterday. Briefly: in a townlet some twenty miles from the French border, the car ruptured a vital organ. So, to get some quiet and avoid being run over in absence of mind, I went into a barber's, forgetting that I'd had my hair cut only the day before, with the result that I am now mowed all but bald. I did not wake up to what was happening until the man started on my eyebrow, probably mistaking it for a supplementary moustache because it turns up at the end in the Mephistelian manner. As it is, I am cropped to the white, like a fox terrier. I shall not feel romantic about you again for at least ten seconds. If the sun is shining in Savoy, and you are motoring much, ask the chauffeur to give you some lubricating oil to rub on your countenance. If you don't it will peel. *I* use a skin food; but engine oil is cheaper and equally effective.

CAMPBELL. You don't deserve to be as clever as you are and it's not that you are *so* clever—it's just your exuberant and mischievous mind. I cannot keep up the exuberance like you, *and* the beloved Irish accent, which I believe the serpent had or Eve would never have noticed the apple. Do something quickly or I shall have vanished. I miss you dreadfully—and Liza, too.

SHAW. Nearer my goddess to thee by another one hundred and twenty miles. Strangely enough I have never been here in Orleans before. I should like to do a Joan of Arc play some day, beginning with the sweeping up of the cinders after her martyrdom and going on with her arrival in Heaven. One of my scenes will be Voltaire and Shakespeare running down side streets to avoid meeting her. Would you like to play the maid? You would come in on horseback in shining armour and fight innumerable supers!

CAMPBELL. Your letters are a carnival of words. How can I answer with my poor whining beggars? It will be dreadful when you realize the commonplace, witless charwoman I really am. And you with so many "great women" about you now, Saint Joan and all. If you are back next Monday or Tuesday, will you come at 4 o'clock and make me laugh and convince me it's worthwhile getting well?

SHAW. Alas, although I am back in England I shall not be within reach of you on Monday or Tuesday, I have to go up to Liverpool and see them through another rehearsal of Caesar and Cleopatra. It was a specially disastrous dress rehearsal. Such dryings-up and wrong cues were

never heard. To my taste the climax was reached when
the end of the fourth act was approaching and the stage
was darkened for the discovery of the murdered Ftateeta.
Cleopatra said "It is dark and I am lonely" with such
convincing naturalness that the sympathetic electrician
consoled her instantly with a flood light which deluged
the stage.

CAMPBELL. Oh darling!—it's too late to do anything
but *accept* you and *love* you—but when you were quite
a little boy somebody ought to have said "hush" just
once. I haven't said "kiss me" because life is too short
for the kiss my heart calls for . . . Look into my eyes
for two minutes without speaking if you dare! Then how
many hours would you be late for dinner?

SHAW. If I looked into your eyes without speaking for
two minutes—*Silent for two minutes with an audience
even of one! Impossible cried the fiend*—I might see
heaven. I think you are getting well. I hear a ring. I see
a flash. The able courageous Stella is stirring. Stella! Who
is Stella? A woman, well, can she love a human dredger?
That's what I am! Does she want to clasp brass to her
bosom—oh, her bosom! I remember now—the jade!—
when she first took my hand she shook it so that it
touched her bosom, an infamous abandoned trick; it
thrilled through me, through all my brass for hours. I
was young and foolish then and could be thrilled. What
did she care for me then? What was my knuckle to her
—it caught me just on the knuckle— Had she felt what
I felt she would have risen up into the skies and set me
there at her right hand. Oh you must, you must be torn
out of your bed and shaken into rude health. Or else I
will get into the bed myself and we shall perish together
scandalously.

CAMPBELL. There are parts of your letters I cannot
reply to. You might lend me some bacteria? The doctors
can't find any in my blood and they want some to cook
and replace— They say now a horse's would do, but I
would so much rather have yours. Oh! I long for you to

be here and throw all three doctors out the window.—If you don't come to see me soon, there won't be a "me" to see!—Ask Charlotte to be kind. (*On the word "Charlotte,"* SHAW *rises quickly and begins to shush her, crossing to her at the same time. She lowers her voice.*) Even if she does think me a lunatic or an adventuress, she might let you call on me while I'm ill. That's perfectly respectable. And I can be terribly proper.

SHAW. (*Standing close to her.*) No. It is best to ask Charlotte nothing; I barely mention your name.—Yesterday a tragedy occurred. She overheard our telephone conversation and the effect was dreadful; I must, it seems, murder myself or else murder her. Well, I daresay, it is good for us all to suffer; but it is hard that the weak should suffer the most. I throw my desperate hands to heaven and ask why one cannot make one beloved woman happy without sacrificing another.

CAMPBELL. I had a dream about Charlotte last night. She shook hands with me warmly and smiled and said, "I thought you were a bird of paradise but you are only a silly goose." The dream ended with my jumping out of bed and taking a taxi to—your house. Stella, la dangereuse. (*She takes her feet off footstool and addresses audience.* SHAW *goes behind his desk and stands looking off.*) After that, I began to recover—I went into a nursing home where they pummeled me in the mornings and strapped me on a board at night; but by January I was able to move about and in February visitors were let come in to see me—and they came by the scores—all the people I knew in London and some I didn't. One came every day bringing roses and gaiety into my room. George Cornwallis-West. It wasn't long before Mr. Shaw noticed his visits and then began to act very peculiarly indeed.

SHAW. (*Turning to her.*) Can it be true? My sprite tells me you are jilting me! Am I spurned indeed? Must I stop making verses? Though I confess I can think of no rhyme for "Stella" but "umbrella" and "too damn *well*" I love "Mrs. Camp*bell*," and horrors of that sort.

Though I like George I say he is young and I am old.
So let him wait until I am tired of you.

CAMPBELL. Be calm, dearest Joey, be gentle with fools.
Poor you. Awful as it is, it is nothing compared to the
humiliation I feel with Charlotte while I am without
husband. Now I know there is nothing you can do about
that, but there is a great deal George can do. So, please!—
But enough of that! I have just heard of the illness of
your beloved mother. I remember you once said, "It is
from her I derive my brains and character which does her
credit." Oh Joey! I know how devotedly you love her.
If she leaves us, it will be a great loss.

SHAW. . . . Mamma, yes! She cut a wisdom tooth
when she was eighty! and now it is the end, they say.
The world is changing horribly . . . G.B.S. (*He crosses
dejectedly around* R. *side of desk.*)

CAMPBELL. I have just been told the sad news. May
she rest in peace!—I had a mother who loved Dante . . .
and whose soul was steeped in beauty. When you can, let
me hear from you.

SHAW. (*There is the minimum of movement in this
speech. The middle section should be almost to himself
as if he were still there in the crematorium. The whole
is filled with* love *for his mother.*) 22nd February, 1913
. . . What a day! I must write to you about it, because
there is no one else who didn't hate her mother, and
even who doesn't hate her children. Whether you are an
Italian peasant or a Superwoman I cannot yet find out:
but anyhow your mother was not the Enemy . . . Why
does a funeral always sharpen one's sense of humor and
rouse one's spirits? This one was a complete success. No
burial horrors. No mourners in black, snivelling and
wallowing in induced grief. Nobody knew except myself,
Granville Barker, and the undertaker. Since I could not
have a splendid procession with lovely colors and flashing
life and triumphant music, it was best with us three. I
particularly mention the undertaker because the humor
of the occasion began with him. I walked to the Crema-

torium with Barker: and there came also the undertaker presently with his hearse, which the horse had walked conscientiously at a funeral pace through the cold; though my mother would have preferred an invigorating trot. The undertaker approached me in the character of a man shattered with grief: and I, hard as nails (rejoicing irrepressibly in my mother's memory), tried to convey to him that this professional chicanery, as I took it to be, was quite unnecessary. And lo! It wasn't professional chicanery at all. He had done all sorts of work for her for years, and was actually and really in a state about losing her . . . And the coffin was covered with violet cloth—not black . . . I must rewrite that burial service; there are things in it that are deader than anyone it has been read over; still with all its drawbacks it is the most beautiful thing that can be read as yet. And the parson did not gabble in the horrible manner common on such occasions. With Barker and myself for his congregation (and Mamma) he did it with his utmost feeling and sincerity. At the passage "earth to earth, ashes to ashes, dust to dust" there was a little alteration of the words to suit the process. A door opened in the wall: and the violet coffin mysteriously passed out through it and vanished as it closed. People think that door the door of the furnace: but it isn't. I went behind the scenes at the end of the service and saw the *real* thing. People are afraid to see it; but it is *wonderful*. I found there the violet coffin opposite another door, a *real* unmistakable furnace door this time: when it lifted there was a plain little chamber of cement and fire-brick. No heat, no noise. No roaring draught. No flame. No fuel. It looked cool, clean, sunny. You would have walked in or put your hand in without misgiving. Then the violet coffin moved again and went in, feet first. And behold! The feet burst miraculously into streaming ribbons of garnet colored lovely flame, smokeless and eager, like pentecostal tongues, and as the whole coffin passed in it sprang into flame all over; and my mother became that beautiful

fire. . . . The door fell; well, they said that if we wanted
to see it all through to the end, we should come back in
an hour and a half. I remembered the wasted little figure
with the wonderful face, and said, "Too long" to myself
—but off we went. . . . When we returned, the end was
wildly funny, Mama would have enjoyed it enormously.
We looked down through an opening in the floor. There
we saw a roomy kitchen, with a big cement table and
two cooks busy at it. They had little tongs in their hands,
and they were deftly and busily picking nails and scraps
of coffin handles out of Mama's dainty little heap of ashes
and samples of bone. Mama herself being at that moment
leaning over beside me, shaking with laughter. Then
they swept her up into a sieve, and shook her out: so
that there was a heap of dust and a heap of bone scraps.
And Mama said in my ear, "Which of the two heaps do
you suppose is me?" . . . and that merry episode was the
end, except for making dust of the bone scraps and scat-
tering them on a flower bed. . . . O grave, where is thy
victory? . . . And so good night, friend, who understands
about one's mother, (*He turns directly to her*.) and *other*
things. Good night.

CAMPBELL. (*She looks at him for a moment then she
gets up and addresses audience.*) Then quite suddenly the
physicians who attended me—the two knights and the
baronet—pronounced me well.

SHAW. (*To audience.*) And Pygmalion was announced
at last for April, 1914.

CAMPBELL. (*To audience.*) I knew myself and my
strength. I needed to go away for a bit to sort things
out. I knew I was too old for Eliza and I had naturally
heard, as who hadn't? the rumours about Joey's be-
haviour at rehearsals; how he bullied his actors mer-
cilessly until he got what he wanted. And I knew I must
be thoroughly prepared. But there was a personal reason,
too, for me to be out of London just now; my "every-
day visitor" George Cornwallis-West. I was beginning
to feel a great "understanding" was growing between us

and in a moment of weakness I said he could come with me to the seaside and hear my lines until rehearsals began. But what to do about Joey? I had had a splinter pulled out from under my nail, he had held my hand. *I used that as an excuse for my note.* (*To* SHAW.) Dear Joey, you were all kindness and sympathy yesterday and I am sure it would have hurt much more if you hadn't been there. Oh, by the way, I'm going down to Sandwich tomorrow for a few days. I want to be alone by the sea and I will hide in the sands somewhere until the play begins. How are strength and steadiness to come to me otherwise, and Eliza? But I must go alone.

SHAW. My dearest love, solitude is wonderful but not when you are alone! Are you very low in the reaction after the pain? If I were with you I would cheat that reaction somehow—hide you from it in my arms—say all sorts of things (all true) to make you forget it. Solitude! When I am solitary you are always with me. When you are solitary by the sea where shall I be? Shall I come?

CAMPBELL. When you are tender like this a thousand cherubs peep out from your purple and black wings. It's getting difficult not to love you more than I ought to love you. Offend me quickly to pull me together again—but don't come here!

SHAW. (*To audience.*) But how could I stay in London now she was herself again? I quickly packed my bag, caught the next train from Victoria and shortly after lunch I was running along the sands to her hotel, singing all the way.

CAMPBELL. He came bounding up the stairs of the hotel just as I was coming down—alone—into the hall. (*They walk towards each other.* SHAW *holds out his arms.*) Joey! What on earth are you doing here? Didn't you read my letter? Please, will you go back to London at once? AT ONCE! (*Pause, while they stare at one another.*) Very well, if you won't go, I will. One of us must behave like a gentleman! Joey, please! (*To audi-*

ence.) But he wouldn't go. I saw him again that evening for dinner, without George, of course, and at eleven o'clock, overcome with sleepiness, to get him back to his hotel, I agreed to go bathing first thing next morning. But it was only a ruse. When he appeared bathing costume and all, we had already driven away, leaving a note with the chambermaid. . . .

SHAW. (*Reading note which he has taken out of his pocket during her speech.*) "When you get this I will have gone. Goodbye. I am still very tired. It was you who should have gone. You were more fit for a journey than I. Stella." Very well, go! The loss of a woman is not the end of the world. The sun shines; it is pleasant to swim; it is good to work; my soul can stand alone! But I am deeply, deeply, deeply wounded. You have no nerve, you have no brain. There is nothing really frank in our comradeship after all. You run after life furtively and when it turns and opens its arms to you you run away. Go then. The Shavian oxygen burns up your little lungs: seek some stuffiness that suits you. You have wounded my vanity. That is the unpardonable crime! You don't care! No you don't. You won't marry George; at the last minute you will funk him or be ousted by a bolder soul. Even if *I* had been secretly bored to distraction I would have stayed on in torment rather than have dealt *you* the enormous blow of *deserting* you. Bah! What do you know of such things? You! Why, you could tear the strings out of an archangel's harp to tie up parcels!

CAMPBELL. Stop. Stop. You vagabond, you blind man, you. You weaver of words . . . you poor thing unable to understand a mere woman. You lost me because you never found me. I said I'd behave like a gentleman and I did. You in your broom-stick and sheet! You smother me with your bellows of self and your egotistical snortings!

SHAW. But you promised! What did you want, oysters and champagne? Well, I've got something out of the trip anyway; I've written the play already: Act one; Stella says Let us bathe before breakfast at a quarter to eight

and George Bernard Shaw says No, at eight! Too late!
Make it quarter to eight! Please, not before eight!
Curtain to act one!! Act Two: Joey comes to bathe.
Smiling chambermaid comes out. They've gone sir. What?
Today? Ha. Ha. I thought it was tomorrow. What a
charming voice and smile that old sport has. *He* don't
care! Curtain! He does care though. Oh Stella, why did
you go? How could you go? Useless these letters, the
wound will not heal! (*He sits looking Offstage.*)

CAMPBELL. But don't you remember? When the waiter
brought the ginger beer he said, "You have already paid
your bill, so the ginger beer will be one shilling." I thought
that you would have guessed then that I was going since
I had paid the bill. But you were too sleepy. I owe you
a shilling! Why do you go on scolding me for the woman
I am and not the woman you would have me be. Do you
think it was nothing to me to hurt my friend? Joey, dear,
don't be hurt. Please, *please*, PLEASE. (*She sits.*)

SHAW. (*After a pause.*) 31st December, 1913 . . .

CAMPBELL. In the New Year may you play with the
moon and kiss the stars—and the earth lie in your lap—

SHAW. O, night of all nights in the year— Do you remember last New Year's Eve? I am actually asking you
do you remember it? Was it anything to you except that
you were ill? *I* remember it; it tears me all to pieces. I
believe we were both well *then,* and have been ill ever
since. For what is this senseless walking about, this business, this repainting and repapering, but disease and mad-
ness? *On that last New Year's Eve* and all the eves that
went before it, there was Eternity and Beauty, infinite,
boundless loveliness and content. I think of it with a
tragic despair: for you have wakened the latent tragedy
in me, broken through my proud over-bearing gaiety that
carried all the tragedies of the world like feathers and
stuck them in my cap and laughed. And if your part in it
was an illusion, then am I as lonely as God. Therefore you
must still be the Mother of Angels to me, still from time
to time put on your divinity and sit in the heavens with

me. For that, with all our assumed cleverness is all **we** two are really fit for. Remember this always, for in this I am deeply faithful to you— Be faithful to me in it and I will forgive you though you betray me in everything else—forgive you, bless you, honor you and adore you. *Super hanc stellam* will I build my Church. And now let us again hear the bells ring: you on your throne in your blue hood, and I watching and praying, not on my knees, but at my fullest stature. For you I wear my head nearest the skies. (*He crosses near her chair during latter part of speech and puts out his hand on final line.*)

CAMPBELL. (*She takes his hand.*) Oh, Joey! If I could write letters like you, I would write letters to God . . . (*They drop hands. She picks up script of* Pygmalion, *rises and thumbs through it.*)

SHAW. (*To audience.*) Pygmalion begins at last: After all the talking and waiting we began rehearsals at His Majesty's Theatre in the middle of February, 1914, with Mrs. Patrick Campbell as Eliza and Sir Herbert Beerbohm Tree as Higgins. The battle lines were drawn and there was no turning back.

CAMPBELL. (*To* SHAW *as she holds script.*) Oh goodness, we're in for it—and let's be *very* clever—I'll be tame as a mouse and oh, so obedient—I wonder if you'll get what you want out of me, I feel a little afraid.

SHAW. (*To audience.*) And indeed we all had reason to be apprehensive . . . Stella, at the age of 49, was asked to play a girl still in her teens . . . and with a cockney accent, at that. . . . And now, the heavy work started— (*He moves* D. R. *chair to* C.) After the first reading we began to rehearse it scene by scene. . . . Now, Stella, as you know the play begins under the arches of St. Paul's Church in Covent Garden. . . . As it is a drizzly London night, several persons are sheltering here— waiting for their cars after the evening's performance at the Opera. Among them, the celebrated professor, Henry Higgins, the world's foremost authority on phonetics. . . . And, amid the general hubbub, we gradually become aware of your voice, Stella, as you approach— (*She begins to pantomime selling violets.*) coming in out of the rain, a slovenly, bedraggled flower girl, Eliza Doolittle. . . .

CAMPBELL. (*As* ELIZA.) Baw ya flah orf a por gal!

SHAW. Higgins springs to attention and whips out his pencil!

CAMPBELL. (*As* ELIZA.) Voylets . . . Voylets . . . who'll buy my voylets?

SHAW. You drop a bunch in the muddy street and seeing them ruined, cry . . .

CAMPBELL. (*As* ELIZA. *She pantomimes dropping bunch and picking it up.*) Ah-ah-aw-aw-oooo. . . .

SHAW. Higgins writes furiously, "What a sound!—what a delicious sound!"

CAMPBELL. (*As* ELIZA.) 'Ere now! Whatcher tiken dawn . . . I'm a good gal, I am—I ain't done nuffink.

SHAW. No, no—Stella—"I ain't done nuffink"— Read it as if you think you're talking to a policeman, not a doctor—try it again.

BOTH. I ain't done nuffink.

SHAW. That's better.

CAMPBELL. I shall die over this accent, anyway— You wrote her a cockney just to torment me.

SHAW. Stella!

CAMPBELL. Oh very well. . . . (*As* ELIZA *truculently.*) —'Ere now. Whatcher takin' down—I'm a good gal, I am. (*She stops.*)

SHAW. Well— Go on.

CAMPBELL. Go on what?

SHAW. You have a cry.

CAMPBELL. What for?

SHAW. Because Higgins has a reply.

CAMPBELL. (*Obliging him.*) Ah-ah-ah-oooo.

SHAW. Thank you. (*As* HIGGINS.) Woman! Cease this detestable boohooing instantly or else seek shelter elsewhere.

CAMPBELL. (*As* ELIZA.) I've a right to be here if I

like, same as you. (*She sits on chair he has placed* s. c.)

SHAW. (*As* HIGGINS.) A woman who utters such depressing and disgusting sounds has no right to be anywhere—no right to live. Remember that you are a human being with a soul and the divine gift of articulate speech; that your native language is the language of Shakespeare and Milton and The Bible; (CAMPBELL *is making cooing sounds, as if whimpering.*) and don't sit there crooning like a bilious pigeon.

CAMPBELL. (*As* ELIZA.) Ah-ah-aw-aw-OOOO . . .

SHAW. (*As* HIGGINS.) You see this creature with her kerbstone English! Well, sir, in six months, I could pass that girl off as a duchess at an ambassador's garden party.

CAMPBELL. (*As* ELIZA.) What's that you say?

SHAW. (*As* HIGGINS.) Yes, you squashed cabbage leaf, you incarnate insult to the English language: I could pass you off as the Queen of Sheba.

CAMPBELL. (*As* ELIZA. *Happily.*) Ah-ah-aw-aw-oo-oo. . . . (*She relapses into* D. R. *chair.*)

SHAW. Well, now, that's not so hard is it, Stella? We might begin to get it in a month or so— (*Crossing back to his desk.*) I am amazed you find it so difficult to be common . . .

CAMPBELL. Well! You've already made me feel thoroughly uncomfortable and this is only the fourth day—you'd better let Charlotte know you are going to make silk purses out of a sow's ears. . . . I'm sorry if I'm difficult. . . . (*Crosses towards her desk.*) But you must admit Eliza is a little more of a lady at the tea scene than you seem to allow.

SHAW. Exactly—what I have written is one-half a lady and one-half a slut, but you are trying to look a slut and play a lady. . . . It simply won't work. And what is the reason for that new "turn away" that's been sneaking in lately?

CAMPBELL. Sneaking in? I like that! I've got to do something. . . . All that business you've given Tree simply won't hold up, that's all.

SHAW. And neither will your smile. . . . Why do you think I gave Tree the apple in the first place?

CAMPBELL. Tree takes five minutes between each word and each bite of that apple! I have a facial paralysis from trying to express any sort of intelligent feeling. That's why I turn away . . . I'm simply hiding my face till it's well again. (*She turns and walks* U.S.)

SHAW. Then that is why your face looks like a burst paper bag! (*He crosses away.*)

CAMPBELL. Don't think you're hurting me—not at all. . . . What you think of me and my poor talent, I am not concerned with now.

SHAW. The "at home" scene still worries me a little— I'll come over to your house in Kensington Square tonight and go over it with you—you still make it too much like a music-hall turn.

CAMPBELL. You've written a music-hall turn!

SHAW. Thank you!

CAMPBELL. And you need all the laughs you can get in your play.

SHAW. Now, then—we'll start after you've arrived and sat down . . . (*He takes her chair and moves it to* C. *so the two chairs are now side by side.*) The others are on each side of you—Mrs. Eynsford Hill here, Freddy there, Mrs. Higgins there. . . . (*She walks in.*) Mrs. Higgins says . . . "Will it rain, do you think?" (*They both sit.*)

CAMPBELL. (*As* ELIZA. *Enunciating.*) The shallow depression in the west of these islands moves slowly in an easterly direction—there are no indications of any great change in the barometrical situation.

SHAW. (*As* FREDDIE.) Oh, I say! Ha! Ha!

CAMPBELL. (*As* ELIZA.) What are you sniggering about, young man? I bet I got it right. . . .

SHAW. (*As* MRS. HIGGINS.) I do hope it won't turn cold. There's so much influenza about.

CAMPBELL. (*As* ELIZA.) My aunt died of influenza, so they said.

SHAW. (As MRS. HIGGINS.) Really!

CAMPBELL. (As ELIZA.) But, it's my belief, they done the old woman in.

SHAW. (As MRS. HIGGINS.) Done her in!

CAMPBELL. (As ELIZA.) Ye-e-s, Lord love you! Why should she die of influenza? She come through diphtheria right enough, the year before. . . . Fairly blue with it, she was. They all thought she was dead. . . . But my father, he kept ladling gin down her throat till she come to so sudden that she bit the bowl off the spoon. What call would a woman with that strength in her have to die of influenza? And what become of her new straw hat that should have come to me? . . . Somebody pinched it; and what I say is, them as pinched it, done her in.

SHAW. (As MRS. EYNSFORD HILL.) You surely don't believe that your aunt was killed?

CAMPBELL. (As ELIZA.) Do I not? Them she lived with, would have killed her for a hat-pin, let alone a hat.

SHAW. (As MRS. HIGGINS.) But it can't have been right for your father to pour spirits down her throat like that. It might have killed her.

CAMPBELL. (As ELIZA.) Not her. Gin was mother's milk, to her. Besides, he'd poured so much down his own throat, that he knew the good of it.

SHAW. (As MRS. HIGGINS.) Good Heavens!

CAMPBELL. (As ELIZA.) It never did him no harm, what I could see. But then he did not keep it up regular. On the burst as you might say. . . .

SHAW. Cheerfully, Stella, cheerfully . . . "On the burst!"

BOTH. On the burst, as you might say, from time to time. And always more agreeable when he had a drop in!

CAMPBELL. (As ELIZA.) Well, I'm afraid I must be going. Goodbye, Mrs. Higgins.

SHAW. (As MRS. HIGGINS.) Goodbye.

CAMPBELL. (As ELIZA.) Goodbye, Mrs. Eynsford Hill.

SHAW. (As MRS. EYNSFORD HILL.) Goodbye.

CAMPBELL. (As ELIZA.) Goodbye, all.

SHAW. (*As* FREDDIE.) If you are walking across the Park, Miss Doolittle, may I . . .

CAMPBELL. (*As* ELIZA.) Walk!? Not bloody likely! I'm going home in a taxi.

SHAW. By George, Stella, we've got it. . . . You can be wonderful when you really try. Goodnight! (*He puts his chair back in place at end of this speech.*)

CAMPBELL. Joey, there's only four days to go. . . . But I'm afraid it isn't *right* enough.

SHAW. *No,* it's not. It's at the end of the play, that's where you still go off. You can boil a scene in bread and milk better than anyone I know, but this would be better boiled in brandy. Perhaps it might help if you could imagine Higgins to be me, then you could be properly scornful. And remember to speak up. Sometimes at the back of the theatre I can't hear a word you say.

CAMPBELL. I know my performance is a mere masquerade, and I've told you from the beginning that I'm years too old for the part and I can't do a cockney to "save me neck." But I can be heard in any theatre in the world, no matter what may be the matter with your ears!

SHAW. Final Orders! Tonight is the night! A great deal will depend on whether you are inspired at the last moment. You are not, like me, a great general. I don't like fighting, I like conquering. But you think you like fighting and now you will have to succeed, sword in hand; and the wonderful thing, Stella, is that I know you will; succeed with dash and brilliancy and resolution. And so . . .

TOGETHER. Avanti!

CAMPBELL. (*To audience.*) The play went like a dream, it was filled with heavenly laughter. Surely no first night in the world had ever gone so joyously.

SHAW. (*To audience.*) With each act the laughter and the applause became louder and more enthusiastic until by the end it was apparent that Stella had taken the whole of London by storm and we were both pitched overnight to the very top of the heap. A celebration had been arranged after the opening. But when I went to fetch Stella, I was in for a shock. Oh! She had a knack for dramatic timing. I found her on the point of leaving the stage door.

CAMPBELL. (*She is startled to see* SHAW.) Joey . . .

SHAW. Aren't you going to the party? You're not going home . . . alone . . . tonight?

CAMPBELL. I'm not going alone. I'm going home with George. He's waiting for me in his motor car.

SHAW. George?

CAMPBELL. Yes. George Cornwallis-West. I married him last Wednesday.

CURTAIN

ACT TWO

At Rise: *LIGHTS up. There has been a slight rearrangement of the furniture to underline the feeling of distance in this act. Enter* CAMPBELL. *She comes slowly* D. C.

CAMPBELL. Pygmalion was the great success of the London season. But the year was 1914. A few months after the opening Belgium was invaded by Germany and all Europe was plunged into war. The theatres in London were closed. Both my husband and my son, Beo, had enlisted and were with the fighting forces at the front. I decided to take Pygmalion to America. Mr. Shaw, as usual so far ahead of the times as to be called traitor by much of the nation, was writing for the New Statesman: (*She crosses a little* S. L.)

SHAW. (*Enter* SHAW; *as if dictating he walks to his desk.*) We must lend our minds to the problem of how to redraw the map of Europe and reform its political constitutions so that this abominable and atrocious nuisance, a European war, shall not easily occur again. (*He sits on his stool.*)

CAMPBELL. (*To audience.*) Then his letters and Beo's letters began getting through to me in New York—before America was in the war. (*She goes to her chair and sits.*)

SHAW. Stella, this war is getting too silly for words, They make no headway and produce no result except kill, kill, kill. The Kaiser asks from time to time for another million men to be killed; and Kitchener asks for another million men to kill them. And now that they have settled the fact that their stupid fighting can't settle anything, and produces nothing but a perpetual Waterloo that nobody wins, why don't the women rise up and say, "We have the trouble of making these men; and if you don't stop killing them we shall refuse to make any

32

more"? But alas, the women are just as idiotic as the men. . . . And that is all, Stella. Might be a scrap of newspaper, might it not? Do you never ask yourself what has become of my sonnets?

CAMPBELL. No, I don't miss your sonnets!—or your love making. I know you so well, Joey—just how much you appreciated me—and how little. I was out of pocket $7,750.00 getting the play across the country to San Francisco, in the sweltering heat and the one-night stands in the practically empty theatres. The people thought Bernard Shaw "highbrow stuff" and wouldn't come near you! . . . They expressed great disappointment that we never spoke the title of the play; they wanted so much to know how it should be pronounced, whether Pyge-malion—or PIG-ma-lion! . . . I have grown quite plain and my hair is getting gray, but then the newspapers in this country are enough to make us all maniacs. A few Sundays ago in enormous headlines "British Navy Sunk." . . . I have been and am very anxious about my son Beo. He got ill in the trenches at the Dardanelles and was sent to Alexandria; only three men left out of his platoon; O, the enormity and eternal bloody error of this war! . . . I miss you very much; I wonder whether I will ever see you again. Stella.

SHAW. I returned from Ireland with the survivors of the *Lusitania* to lecture on the London platform about the war. Your latest photograph is too young and beautiful to be true; you should see *me*. I look seventy. The theatre is passing away from me as a sort of wild oats: I go back to politics, religion and philosophy. They give me frightful headaches, but satisfy my soul.

CAMPBELL. (*To audience.*) After two long years in America, I returned in 1916 to London for George Alexander's revival of *BELLA DONNA*. My husband had escaped from Antwerp, but Beo had been sent back to the front. The war was getting more horrible every day—the casualty lists—the wounded in the streets! It was months before I heard from Joey again.

SHAW.
Ayot St. Lawrence;
14th May 1916

I have had influenza, and in spite of a fortnight by the
sea, I feel suicidal. My new volume should have been
out a month ago, but there was no labor to print it, no
labor to bind it, and no good train taking less than three
months to come to London from Edinburgh, where my
printing is done. The sequel to Pygmalion is on page 191.
It will not interest you; but George will read it. I assume
that you are in London; but I don't care: I never felt
so morose in my life. I can't write: nothing comes off but
screeds for the papers, mostly about this blasted war. I
am old and finished. I am creeping through a new play
(to prevent myself crying) at odd moments, two or three
speeches at a time. I don't know what it's about. I began
it six months ago and I have hardly come to the beginning
of the first scene yet. This is a rotten world. George looked
tired when he came back: I do not think he has long to
live. You must be feeling very old and feeble. Well,
goodbye: we shall probably never meet again. My address
will soon be, The Crematorium, Golders Green, London.

CAMPBELL. Oh, dear me, as though I didn't know *all*
that years ago! You poor, poor *rich* man. My beloved
Beo is in great danger and my heart aches and the hours
are heavy.

SHAW. 7th March, 1917 . . . You have sent me half
a letter, scrawled in a most uneducated manner. Send
me the rest and I will answer it. What I have seems to
be the last two sheets. Let me have the first six. There
are three depths of illiteracy, each deeper than the one
before. (*Crosses to* U. R. *of her desk.*)
1. The illiteracy of those illiterate enough not to know
   that they are illiterate . . .
2. The illiteracy of Eliza, who couldn't even read the
   end of her own story . . .
3. The illiteracy of those who have never read my
   works . . .

There is only one person alive who is such a monster of illiteracy as to combine these three illiteracies in her single brain. And I, the greatest living Master of Letters, made a Perfect Spectacle of myself with her before all Europe. (*He turns away.*)

CAMPBELL. My beloved Beo is killed— You have seen it in the papers. I feel he is asleep and will wake and come to me if I am quite strong and calm. . . . Do you think MacDona would like me to play Eliza in the big towns with him? . . . The chaplain writes that Beo and the Commanding Officer were standing at the top of the stairs of their dugout when a shell burst and killed them both instantaneously— I would like you to read the letter. It is full of tragic gentleness and praise of my brave son.

SHAW. It is no use: I cannot be sympathetic: these things simply make me furious. I want to swear. I *do* swear. Killed just because people are blasted fools. A chaplain, too, to say nice things about it. It is not his business to say nice things about it, but to shout that "the voice of thy son's blood crieth unto God from the ground." . . . No: don't show me the letter. To hell with your chaplain and his tragic gentleness! The next shell will probably blow *him* to bits; and there will be another chaplain to write such a nice letter to *his* mother. . . . Gratifying, isn't it? Consoling. It only needs a letter from the King to make me feel that shell was a blessing in disguise. . . . No use going on like this, Stella. Wait a week; and then I shall be very clever and broadminded again, and have forgotten all about him. I shall be quite as nice as the chaplain. . . . Oh damn, damn, damn, damn, damn, damn, damn, DAMN. DAMN! . . . And oh, dear, dear, dear, dear, dear.—*Dearest!*—

CAMPBELL. (*To audience.*) If Beo had survived only a short time longer the war would have been over—!

SHAW. With the armistice came a changed world—not politically, of course, but socially and economically— The fashions of King Edward were gone—George V's era was one that began to leave Stella behind; slowly, of course, but with a steady erosion. And our relationship took a tragi-comic turn— We suddenly found ourselves quarreling like blazes over what was to be done with all the letters we'd written to each other and, curiously, seem both to have kept!

CAMPBELL. January 1921 . . . (*To* SHAW. *She is looking through the packet of letters on her desk.*) Joey, I have had a letter from a publisher that I would very much like your opinion upon. It is in the form of a contract for my book and I am afraid of it— Please let me know when you will be in town. A friend from New York writes most enthusiastically about Heartbreak House—it *would* be a little unkind of you to leave me out if it is done here—she says it plays ever so much better than it reads!

SHAW. (*He has crossed to her during her speech.*) Belovedovedest . . . I can't put you into the cast of Heartbreak House. You have intimidated me far too completely during the rehearsals of Pygmalion and the rest of the cast would go on strike at once. What *I* dare not face, nobody else with any sense is likely to take on.

CAMPBELL. I will never get over it— It's such a pity I can't cry.

SHAW. Yes: it is a pity you can't cry. Any actress could.

CAMPBELL. This book business worries me.

SHAW. What have you written? Your life, or mine, or both?

CAMPBELL. You know I can neither write nor spell—neither can I spin,—nor act— My wedding of words is unmoral—and my only idea of notation is a hyphen. Please help me.

SHAW. Very well, Stella, . . . I have settled it! Your book is to be called *The Autobiography of an Enchantress*. . . . I think you will get under way quite easily if, after chronicling The Second Mrs. Tanqueray, you draw a double bar and spend the rest of your story on stage lovers and such like: beginning with Beerbohm Tree, whose evening suit you stroked with passionate embraces of your heavily made up arms until the poor man was like a zebra; and ending with Gerald du Maurier, whose outpourings of admiration on the stage you punctuated by such asides as, "Good God, to have to play a scene like this to a face like that!"

CAMPBELL. Your pen makes you drunk-- I hear Charlotte is distressed! . . . I hope this isn't true— You never told her I was a gentleman or that I was merely swan-singing? . . . It is a pity I ever read these letters again and it's a pity they are so lovely. And I am *glad* I never destroyed them. . . . A copy is being made of the ones that I propose publishing—if you agree.

SHAW. Listen: You say that you will behave like a perfect gentleman. Well, a gentleman does not kiss and tell; so that settles that.

CAMPBELL. It is quite easy for me to come down from the clouds and realize there are other points of view than my own.

SHAW. I have been asked to write some autobiographical sketches for the proposed collected edition of my work. Suppose I put in *your* most intimate letters! Would any plea that I had your leave to do it save me from being put down as an inconceivable cad and coxcomb!

CAMPBELL. Joey—I am going to take you seriously; you say, "Suppose I put in *your* most intimate letters!" . . . You may publish any letters of mine if you will correct the grammar and see to the punctuation.

SHAW. 'ROUND ABOUT 1895 OR SO, I wrote a wonderful string of love letters to Ellen Terry, and got a wonderful string of replies from her . . . and—

CAMPBELL. Why not get Ellen Terry to let me publish her love letters from you, *with* mine?—

SHAW. I quite understand your intense reluctance to let me see the whole book. You are quite right! I shall ruthlessly tear it to pieces. . . .

CAMPBELL. I long for you to see that whole book and to damn it—only not please at Ayot or 10 Adelphi Terrace. . . . It would not take more than two hours to read. I would come up to London. Shall I?

SHAW. I warn you I shall have to connect your titbits into dignified paragraphs, and, where I happen to know the truth, to substitute it for your "dramatization."

CAMPBELL. That's a silly word "dramatization."—I have done my best to be truthful and non-theatrical. . . . You know I cannot write paragraphs—or those glorious long sentences of yours where, when I have arrived at the full stop I have to begin all over again to get my brain's balance!

SHAW. Why, there is one passage on which your George could get a divorce. . . .

CAMPBELL. Let me know that passage.

SHAW. The cruelty of your making me read it!

CAMPBELL. Please, Joey, don't put on your suburban cap. You first said "I leave the publication, etc., to Mrs. Campbell's judgment." Than you're taking it all back.

SHAW. It takes a sledge hammer to knock anything into you that will make you see yourself as others *will* see you. . . .

CAMPBELL. Say as many unkind and cruel things as you like—hit me with a thousand hammers—nobody can hurt me any more: is that not wonderful? Why do you object to the funny silliness of the world a hundred years from now? They will say I was your mistress and the Prince of Wales our son! (*Crosses* D. L.)

SHAW. Now God defend me from idiots! . . . I might just as well write essays on Relativity to a female Kingfisher. . . . Very well! *Send* me your proofs. I will then tell you, brutally and dogmatically, what you may say and what you may not.

CAMPBELL. I wonder how you would have liked to send Shakespeare your first manuscript for him to damn, and his wife, and typist perhaps, to criticize, when he *could* have talked it over with you? I am afraid I am a

little grumpy but perhaps if you had *never* made love to
me I wouldn't mind your disagreeableness now . . . so
please. . . . As to "Relativity," it is a philosophy that
"empties the baby out with the bath water"—that's what
you'll do with my book. (*Sits.*)

SHAW. (*He comes near her and speaks with infinite
patience as if to a child.*) I must talk to you as a child
of nine; you start from the position that the publication
of intimate letters is not permissible among persons of
honour. Now, if these letters are love letters the difficulty
is decupled, centupled, multipled. If they are love letters
from a married man to a woman who is not his wife, and
who is engaged at the time to another man whom she has
subsequently married, the difficulty becomes a wild im-
possibility: if the man publishes them he is a blackguard:
if the woman publishes them, she is a rotter and in the
face of this you keep asking me why you should *not*
publish the letters. You might as well ask me why you
should not pick pockets or sell yourself on the street!

CAMPBELL. I burn so with blushes at your confounded
impudence, that I don't feel the cold. . . . You have
spoilt my book. . . . You have spoilt my story. . . .
You have hidden from the world the one thing that would
have done it good: Lustless lions at play. . . . May you
freeze in that sea of ice in Dante's Inferno—I don't care.
. . . "Stolen your fig-leaf" indeed! You wear no fig-leaf
in your letters. Publishers—money? Rot—! Ugh—

SHAW. Stella, I don't want to hear another word! Do
you know why I took away those letters? Because I
absolutely refuse any longer to play the horse to your
Lady Godiva. (*Crosses* D.R. *and sits on chair, arms
folded.*)

CAMPBELL. There! It is just this epileptic revulsion
that keeps you from being the "Superman" you would be
—and that you think you are. As the letters are now,
they are twaddle. As you sent them back to me they
misrepresented both me and my feelings. I flirted with
no "super-philanderer." That is all lies. I was attached

to what has turned out, a very ordinary individual. I am
going to publish exactly what I like—if you didn't mean
what you wrote, you shouldn't have written it. Be thank-
ful if I cut enough out, and leave enough in, so that you
dare face the public again. Start saying your prayers. I
have your letter giving me absolute permission. So you
be civil. It's no use being a gentleman with you—you've
reneged, that's your game always. And the next time you
try and fascinate an actress, don't use her as a means of
teasing Charlotte—*that* was the ugliest thing you did.
You don't amuse me— "We are not amused." A man who
reneges is . . . well . . . an *Irishman.* (*To audience.*)
The book came out with some of the letters in it, much
cut up, of course, but still "something like" and the press
was wonderful. Everyone said I'd shown the world the
real Shaw, the human Shaw. And what a success he was
having—his plays were all over the place—*Misalliance*
and *Getting Married* and *Heartbreak House* and finally, of
course, *St. Joan.* It was the day after that opened so
triumphantly in London that I heard from him again—
after nearly sixteen months of angry silence.

SHAW. (*He stares stonily out front for a moment before saying.*) Then you still live! (*He looks at her; she
looks at him, rises, crosses up to his desk.*) I went to
Lyall Swete's dressing-room to give him a final word
before the curtain rose; and he began to rave about you
as the greatest actress in the world, swearing that you
are as beautiful as ever, and that you had trained a perfect company to support you in perfect performances of
Hedda Gabler and other plays. The man must be crazy.
. . . So now I forgive you the letters because there is a
star somewhere on which you were right about them:
and on that star we two should have been born. It was
funny how few people knew. . . . Well, are you quite
well? And are you making plenty of money? and has
your virgin loveliness really come back? and do you
remember Tristan and Isolde and forget all our stupid
conflicts? and did the book get you out of debt? and—

and—and—what sort of life are you having generally?
. . . I shall be 68 in July: that is about all my news,
except what you may read in the papers.

CAMPBELL. Dear dear Joey, Your letter at the theatre
gave me strange pleasure. . . . Yes, the book brought
in about £2,500. Will you take me to a matinee of *Saint
Joan* this week? That would make up for a great deal. I
have read your praises with so much pleasure—dear Joey
—that you go deep deep down into the human heart, that
it is far the finest thing that you have ever done, and
you are compared with Mr. Shakespeare, of course, and
in one paper all they said was the youth of you. . . .
Sixty-eight indeed? Twenty-two—and I your grand-
mother. . . . I never forget Tristan and Isolde—harps
in the air.

SHAW. O Lord, Stella, let's not quarrel until we are
both dead. Then we can be added to Heloise and Abelard,
and Romeo and Juliet, and all the rest of them. God
intended you to play the serpent in "Back to Methuselah." I wrote it for your voice. When I told Edith Evans
that she would have to enter bald-headed, old, half naked,
and in rags, in a bevy of youths and maidens made as
pretty as the stage could make them, and that in that
condition as would outfascinate them all and play them
clean out of existence, she believed, and did it. Sybil
Thorndike has never let me forget for a single second
for the last four months, that she considers me as far
superior to the Holy Trinity as a director. And now
Siddons and Rachel were never so praised and exalted
as Thorndike and Evans. If you had only had faith as
much as a grain of mustard seed!

CAMPBELL. You know I feel rather like the little black
girl who after the Englishman kissed her, ran to her
mother and said, "Englishmen eatee me upee," and the
next day crept back to the Englishman and said—"Eatee
me upee some more."

SHAW. (*To audience.*) Stella began to fall on bad days
—for a short time just before the great Depression, she

was reduced to giving lectures on "Diction in Dramatic Art"—and her international reputation as a hellion had far outstripped the facts. But it was becoming harder and harder for her to get new plays—her age was against her, for one thing, and her terms were always high—and her pride higher still.

CAMPBELL. February, 1929. Dear Joey, I was under the impression that the great battle of life was fought in our youth—not a bit of it—it's when we are old, and our work not wanted that it rages and goes on . . . and on . . . and on. . . . My landlord won't allow pupils here, and to take a place to teach in—well, it's too much of a venture. . . . I wonder if you will come and read *your* new play to me as you have half promised you would.

SHAW. I can't read plays to a starving woman, Stella. Oh, what are we to do about you? Why doesn't George give you some help?

CAMPBELL. I thought you knew he left me two years ago!

SHAW. Oh Stella! I know— What about a benefit? Sybil Thorndike says that there are plenty of arists who adored you and would do anything for you. Ellen Terry had a benefit that enabled her to retire and die in comfort. . . .

CAMPBELL. And I don't want a benefit. I sent a cheque for £25 to Ellen Terry's, which she acknowledged with a letter beginning: "Dear Sir." Joey dear,—you who once wrote that you were my "friend world without end"— come and read your play to me. We open next week and after that you can come Thursday, Friday, I am free until 4:30, or Saturday. I am dying to know what it's about.

SHAW. The honest truth is that I am too shy to read you the only scene in that play that would interest you.

CAMPBELL. (*Rises.*) The one scene that would interest me. Now I begin to understand! I went to the Selfridge Ball last night and met Miss Edith Evans, who gazed eagerly at me, saying she was playing me in THE APPLE

CART. Everyone was talking of nothing else . . . the infamy of it . . . and that I must write to you at once —that it is a national calamity, an insult—

SHAW. (*Interrupting.*) Now you must not talk too much. There is of course nothing that could give any clue to the public—above all to the Press. It can be a secret between us.

CAMPBELL. How can it be a "secret" between us— when Edith Evans told me she was playing *me?*

SHAW. Edith Evans guessed of course. Perhaps half a dozen others knew or think they know! for only you and I will ever know; but the press must never get hold of it.

CAMPBELL. No, Joey—if I had the script here I would talk it over with my lawyer—I am in its suggestiveness, it is libelous and ought not to be presented.

SHAW. I don't feel it to be a bit wrong. It plays magnificently.

CAMPBELL. Oh! You *are* a mountebank.

SHAW. Of course! We are a pair of mountebanks: but why oh why do you get nothing out of me, though I get everything out of you? Mrs. Hesione Hushabye in *Heartbreak House*, the Serpent in *Methuselah*, whom I always hear speaking with your voice, and Orinthia: all you, to say nothing of Eliza, who was only a joke. You are the Vamp and I the victim; yet it is I who suck your blood and fatten on it whilst you lose everything! . . . But I am as right about this play as you were about the letters—you will see— "My Dearest Liar" is there for all the world to love as I did. . . . I will come to your house tonight and we will read the scene aloud, together. You might be surprised at its purity after all the fuss. (*Crosses to* STELLA *with script.*) Here is the script— Orinthia you are, it is a reminiscence of our afternoons in Kensington Square in the old days. The scene is in Orinthia's boudoir. . . . (*He moves her chair out to* C.) You are at the writing table scribbling notes. Romantically beautiful and beautifully dressed--

CAMPBELL. That's something!

SHAW. King Magnus enters and waits on the threshold. . . . You say . . .

CAMPBELL. (*She is very reluctant and suspicious. She glares at him before commencing.* ORINTHIA.) Who is that? (*She sits to read.*)

SHAW. (*In order to please her he overdoes his part.* MAGNUS.) His Majesty, the King.

CAMPBELL. (ORINTHIA.) Tell the King I don't want to see him.

SHAW. (MAGNUS.) He awaits your pleasure— He comes down and sits. (*He brings his chair over and places it near her, at* L.)

CAMPBELL. (ORINTHIA. *Without any hint of characterization.*) Go away.—A pause.—I wont speak to you.— Another pause. . . . If my private rooms are to be broken into at any moment because they are in the Palace and the King is not a gentleman, I must take a house outside.

SHAW. (MAGNUS.) What is our quarrel today, beloved?

CAMPBELL. (ORINTHIA.) Ask your conscience.

SHAW. (MAGNUS.) I have none when you are concerned. You must tell me.

CAMPBELL. (ORINTHIA.) There. Look at this book.— She shows him the book.

SHAW. (MAGNUS.) What is this?

CAMPBELL. (ORINTHIA.) Read the first three words . . . if you dare.

SHAW. (MAGNUS.) "Orinthia, my beloved."

CAMPBELL. (ORINTHIA.) The name you pretended to invent especially for me. . . . You are the King of Liars and Humbugs. . . . (*As herself.*) Not bad, that.

SHAW. Just read the lines.

CAMPBELL. She turns away.

SHAW. The lines! You needn't read the directions!

CAMPBELL. Your line.

SHAW. (*Reading.*) She turns aw—! And don't pretend

to be hurt unless you really are, dearest. It wrings my heart. . . .

CAMPBELL. (ORINTHIA.) Since when have you set up a heart? Did you buy that too, second-hand? (*As herself.*) This is your best play, Joey. (*As* ORINTHIA.) Listen to me, Magnus. Why can you not be a real king?

SHAW. (MAGNUS.) In what way, belovedest?

CAMPBELL. (ORINTHIA.) What you need to make you a real king is a real queen.

SHAW. (MAGNUS.) But I have got one.

CAMPBELL. (ORINTHIA.) Oh, you are blind. You are worse than blind: you have low tastes. (*As herself.*) That's true enough. Heaven is offering you a rose; and you cling to a cabbage. (*As herself.*) Is that nice to Charlotte, Joey?

SHAW. (*As himself.*) It's a very apt metaphor, beloved. (MAGNUS.) But what wise man, if you force him to choose between doing without roses and doing without cabbages, would not secure the cabbages? Besides, you should know better than anyone else that when a man gets tired of his wife and leaves her, it is never because she has lost her good looks. The new love is often older and uglier than the old.

CAMPBELL. (*As* ORINTHIA *but warningly.*) Why should I know it better than anyone else?

SHAW. (MAGNUS. *Blandly.*) Why, because you have been married twice; and both your husbands have run away from you to much plainer and stupider women.

CAMPBELL. (ORINTHIA.) Shall I tell you why these men could not live with me? It was because I was higher than they were, and greater, they could not stand the strain of trying to live up to me.

SHAW. (MAGNUS.) Good lord! It must be magnificent to have the consciousnes of a godess without ever doing anything to justify it.

CAMPBELL. All of this is ridiculous, Joey! *Pat* never left me. He died!

SHAW. (*Himself.*) Orinthia's husbands are not Pat or

George. They are simply suggested by all the millions of men, who bit off more than they could chew.

CAMPBELL. Rot, this is a dreadful play.

SHAW. Please go on reading, Stella; it was you who asked to read it in the first place.

CAMPBELL. This scene should never have been written.

SHAW. Do you know why I gave this play to Edith Evans and not to you?

CAMPBELL. No, why?

SHAW. Because I knew you would sabotage rehearsals reading it just like that.

CAMPBELL. Do you know what you are, Joey?

SHAW. What?

CAMPBELL. You are what the Greeks call an ampmisbeana.

SHAW. And what is that?

CAMPBELL. A creature, my dear Joey, with a head at each end of its body both walking in different directions. (*As* ORINTHIA.) Magnus, when are you going to face my destiny and your own?

SHAW. (MAGNUS.) But my wife? The Queen? What is to become of my poor dear Jemima?

CAMPBELL. (ORINTHIA.) Oh, drown her: shoot her; tell your chauffeur to drive her into the Serpentine and leave her there. The woman makes you ridiculous.

SHAW. (MAGNUS.) I don't think I should like that. And the public would think it ill-natured.

CAMPBELL. (ORINTHIA.) Oh, you know what I mean. Divorce her. Make her divorce you. It is quite easy. Everyone does it when they need a change.

SHAW. (MAGNUS.) But I can't imagine what I should do without Jemima.

CAMPBELL. (ORINTHIA.) Nobody else can imagine what you do *with* her. (*As herself.*) Really, Joey! (*She throws script down.* SHAW *gives it back.*) All this is preposterous! (*She throws script down again.*)

SHAW. There's only a bit more. Listen. (*He proceeds to read the rest.*) Magnus says, looking at his watch, "now I must go back to my work" and Orinthia says, "What work have you that is more important than being with me?"

"None."

"Then sit down."

"Yes," he says, "but tea is at half-past four."

Detaining him, she says, "Never mind your tea."

"You are only trying to make me late to annoy my wife." He tries to rise but she pulls him back. "Let me go, please."

Orinthia holds on. "Why are you so afraid of your wife, you poor hen-pecked darling?"

"Henpecked! What do you call this? At least my wife does not restrain me by bodily violence." He tries to rise but she pulls him back. "Must I call the guard?"

"Do, do. It will be in all the papers tomorrow."

"Fiend, Orinthia! I command you!" Orinthia laughs wildly: "HA, HA, HA!"

"Very well, you she-devil, you shall let go."

He tackles her in earnest. She flings her arms around him and holds on with mischievous enjoyment; finally dragging him to the floor, where they roll over one another. Suddenly the door is flung open and Sempronius, the first secretary, enters and gazes horror-struck at the scandalous scene as the curtain falls. (*To* CAMPBELL, *who is sitting in awe-struck horror.*) There . . . have I not made a superb picture of you?

CAMPBELL. It's a dreadful thing to have a vaulting mind that o'erleaps itself and goes potty.

SHAW. What?

CAMPBELL. Tear it up. Tear it up and re-write it. People will only say that old age and your super-human vanity have robbed you of your common sense.

SHAW. You dare give yourself airs with me?

CAMPBELL. Yes, Mr. Shaw, I dare! If you went to heaven you would think it funny to shake hands with God and pull the chair out from under him at the same time! (*She goes out.*)

SHAW. (*To audience.*) Then seven years passed—years
in which we both got older and more cantankerous—and
farther apart than ever. (SHAW *replaces his chair.*)
Stella had often been asked to go to Hollywood during
the silent picture era. She had always refused. But with
the advent of the talkies, she thought she might have a
try at it. And off she went—bag, baggage and Pekingese.
Though she had been in America many times and thought
she knew the country pretty well, she was completely
unprepared for the life she found in Southern California.
The Kings and Queens of Hollywood, though stars to all
the world, were only celluloid names to her. And when
she would meet them at the great parties in Beverly Hills,
she simply couldn't resist a jibe. When she met Joan
Crawford, she asked her "what she did." She said to
John Gilbert, the greatest lover of the silent films,
"Young man, you're very good-looking, you should try
to get in the movies." There is the story of her first film
—she appeared on the lot and reported to the director—
he said, "How are you, darling?" She said— "Well enough
—darling, could you tell me what it's all about and we'll
get on with it—?" "All right," he said, his hackles
already up to the moon: "You're the widow of a sea-
faring man—only you don't know it yet—you're still
waiting for him to come back— Now in this scene we'll
take first, you come into the room, shut the door behind
you, cross to the table, pick up a telescope, walk to the
window, open it, raise the telescope to your eye and gaze
steadily out to sea. Do you think you can do that?" She
said she thought she could. "Very well, then, we'll shoot
it—" and he rolled the cameras. Stella came into the
room, closed the door behind her, crossed, picked up the
telescope, went to the window, opened it, raised the telescope—stopped—turned to the director and said: "Which
eye?" Needless to say she wasn't too popular. Her parts
got smaller and smaller and her money ran out. During
all this time she had with her her last and most famous of
all her Pekinese, Moonbeam, and many were the things

she wouldn't do because of him. She wouldn't come back to England at all because of the six-month quarantine law for dogs, and she wouldn't go anywhere Moonbeam couldn't go. Probably the greatest tribute Stella ever paid to this little beast was during a ride in a taxicab one afternoon in Hollywood, when the two of them were seated side by side on the back seat, and Moonbeam suddenly jumped to the floor of the cab and behaved— well—like a dog. When it came time to pay the bill, the driver, on returning her change noticed that the floor of the cab was rather damp. He was about to remonstrate with Stella when she picked Moonbeam up in her arms, looked the man full in the face and said, *"I did it!"* Well, with behavior like that, it's no wonder her stay in Hollywood was rather short-lived. (*He replaces his chair.*) In 1935 I suggested her for a small part in the Theatre Guild production of my new play, *The Millionairess.* But she thought they insulted her and she never went to see them. (*He replaces her chair by her desk.*) In April, 1935, after she'd heard about *The Millionairess* and thinking, (*He walks back towards his desk.*) I'm afraid, that she'd been offered the leading part in it, she wrote from Hollywood. (*Sits on stool.*)

CAMPBELL. (*Enters* U. C. *She gives the address as she slowly walks down around desk and up to window.*) Sunset Tower, Sunset Boulevard, Hollywood, California.

Dear Joey, it was very cheering, and very happy to get your letter. . . . The Theatre Guild with their "subscription list" are a little intolerable; they treat Artists like bales of cotton! . . . I enclose my photograph taken six months ago—you will see I still hold together should you really want me for your *Millionairess*—wouldn't that be wonderful? I wonder what she is like? What sort of things she says and does. Hollywood and the Camera have taught me humility—deep humility: nobody need be afraid of me any more. Three weeks' work in 16 months—think of that misery—it has almost broken me up. . . . The studios say I am too celebrated for small parts, and too English to "star"—that Kalamazoo, Butte, Montana, and Seattle, would not understand my English style and speech. . . . Whenever I ring up my agents they answer: "M.G.M. is thinking of you but nothing suitable has come along."

In retirement in Florence I could get along—but the urge won't be silenced . . . yet! It's odd that I don't mind brazenly cadging from you . . . I am in a very nasty jam—I can go on for six weeks perhaps, but it will be six weeks, perhaps more, before my allowance comes again, and then it won't be enough to put me straight. Will you help me? I don't mind being in the battle to the finish, but in this place one gets left in mid-air. . . . Give a glance at "Moonbeam's" picture—could you have shut him up for 6 months? To him I am a goddess; how could I betray him? . . . Do, dear Joey, take care of yourself and laze a little. . . .

As always, Stella.

SHAW. 11th August 1937. . . . My antiquity, now extreme at eighty-one, has obliged me to make a clearance among my papers and take measures generally for my probably imminent decease. I find that I have done a very wicked thing: I have kept all your letters in spite of my rule never to keep anything but necessary business memoranda. I kept Ellen Terry's because her handwriting made pictures of them which I could not burn; it would have been like burning a XV Century French Book of Hours. I have no such excuse in your case. (*He rises.*) I intended to buy from one of the fashionable lock-smiths a beautiful jewel box big enough to hold the correspondence. But the only safe and easy plan is—just to stuff the letters into a vulgar set of registered envelopes and post them back to you so that you may have the complete correspondence in your hands. This will add to its value if you have to sell it. (*He crosses down, an old man, to the chair.*) I rejoice to learn from the things you said to the Press that you ought not to have said, that you are still Stella. I wish I were still Joey; but I have to be content now to play Pantaloon. . . . (*He sits.*)

CAMPBELL. New York, August, 1937. . . . Dearest Joey, I expect the registered envelopes will soon be here. Oh dear me! There's a clutch at my heart . . . the desire to feel a child again will tempt me to read them. . . . I don't understand why your ashes and Charlotte's ashes have to be scattered over the ground before your letters to me may be published. . . . In 50 years' time life will be lived in the *air*—nobody will read books. But your letters to me will be carried in the airman's luggage because of the thrush in your throat! How it sings in your letters to me. . . . That song will cease if those letters wait 50 years to be published. 81 indeed! Remember the age of the song of the thrush—81 thousand years or more! James Barrie's going makes one pause and so many others—speeding on. B's £500 a year provides for me . . . I live simply in the cheapest hotel in New York—$83 a month—and a refrigerator. I was ill in bed for nearly nine weeks. The dear Irish housemaid used to come in on tiptoe every morning and say in a cheerful voice as I opened my eyes: "Sure and I thought it was dead you were!" John Gielgud, the nephew of your beloved Ellen Terry, found me there and brought me flowers with tears in his eyes. The Terrys weep easily. Now I am quite, *quite* well. I have just returned from playing in two summer theatres—Cohasset and Connecticut. An ovation and a cry for a speech each night were comforting so far as these things go. . . . I don't expect you to answer this letter—I wanted you to know what I had been doing with life these last few years.

SHAW. Before I could answer this touching letter I fell gravely ill—some newspapers in America even announced my death—complete with obituaries and editorials and sighs of relief.

CAMPBELL. Lago di Garda, May 1938. Dear Joey,—It

is miserable to read of your illness in the newspapers. My beloved Italy has done wonders for me—I was carried on the boat when I left the States, and off the boat when I arrived at Boulogne—a rheumatic knee—four months of agony, and the American Doctor has said "18 months and crutches." When the Italian Doctor saw it, he smiled and said: "I will have you dancing in a fortnight"— And sure enough twelve radium-mud packs for twelve days— has completely cured me. . . . But the only thing that matters now is that you should get better—it troubles me very much.

SHAW. (*He rises.*) Stella, this is an age of miracles! (*Crosses back to desk.*) I am back at my desk! . . . The doctors seemed to have cured me at last by stabbing at me in the seat once a fortnight with a monstrous hypodermic syringe. So for the moment I am not dead, though keeping me alive is pure officiousness, as I am 82, and look it. (*Sits on stool.*) Anyway that fellow Hitler will kill us all if the doctors don't.

CAMPBELL. Dear Joey, do cease your comic allusions to age or you'll be missing the glory of the sunset. I've just heard of the huge success of your cinema *Pygmalion* —you must be making more money than you know what to do with. I wonder if you remember all the trouble I took—when was it? Nearly 30 years ago! How I took the play to Tree and begged him to ask you to come and read it to him—and said I would play Eliza— How we all stood your insults at rehearsals! How you nearly killed Tree with that sickly suburban pun, "I say, Tree, must you be so Tree-acly." Of course you have forgotten everything or you would have sent a Christmas box. And you have dared to go about the world saying that *I* am impossible in the theatre . . . because of that one day I couldn't stand it one more minute. (*Rises and advances to front of stage; points into audience.*) I rose, advanced to the footlights and said, "If Mr. Shaw doesn't leave the theatre, I will!" Do you remember that, Joey? It's true, whether you do or not!

SHAW. If only I had time to write your reminiscences for you I'd make you the most famous woman in Europe and America. I haven't any money and I have huge sums to pay the government next month; the cinema *Pygmalion* has not sent a penny my way yet. As to bringing you over, I had as soon bring the devil over. You would upset me and everybody else. You don't know how I have blessed that quarantine law for dogs. . . . If only you could write a true book entitled *Why, Though I Was a Wonderful Actress, No Manager Would Ever Engage Me TWICE if He Could Possibly Help it.*

CAMPBELL. Oh, liar! Liar—dear liar! . . . *six* engagements with Alexander—*nine* engagements with Forbes Robertson—*four* with Gerald du Maurier . . . *two* with Hare—*four* with Tree . . . but what's the use of bothering about your willful nonsense. . . . If war comes what will happen to the letters, I wonder? . . . I've stuffed them all into an old battered hat box and I hide them under the bed at night. So there you are at last, Joey, *under* my bed. I am in one little room here, but I have an open wood fire—and a lovely view over the Tuileries Gardens —and the Parisian sun all day. The covered colonnades go all down the street so I can go out wet or fine. The Duke and Duchess of Windsor live three doors down on my right. He looks tranquil—she looks calm. I see you have another play! At your age!

SHAW. Yes, my new play, *Geneva,* is horrible! The politest critic describes me as a dignified monkey shying coconuts at the audience. I went to see it the other day and it made me quite ill. Splendid for the actors though. The performances are like election meetings. . . . I must stop making myself unpleasant. But I have to write plays like *Geneva.* It is not that I want to. It can't be helped —the war coming and all—Stella, you know, "Joey" was the cleverest thing you ever invented . . . by far, by far, by far.

CAMPBELL. I have invented Joey? Your written words inspired me If they were false, then Joey is an impostor—

But there! I am not going to waste your time with any more of my "ridiculous" letters— We will meet in heaven, you will bow, I will curtsey, and the angels will say to each other: ". . . they did not snatch at joy and spoil the winged world"—

SHAW. (*To audience. An old man.*) I was to hear from Stella only once more—then I wrote to her again a month later. And that was all. Her letter was dated June 28, 1939— It was written just before she went south to Pau where a few months later she died of a sudden illness. Hitler was massing his tanks before the Maginot Line and the Second World War was nearly upon us—I'd already sent word to Stella that they were considering her for a role in the film of my *Major Barbara*, but I wondered if she was still seriously in the field—

CAMPBELL. Yes: I am still seriously "in the field": but not, you know, as cannon fodder. . . . A week or two ago I thought I would be heroic—I offered myself to the English Theatre here at £25 a week, or less. In answer they sent me a play to read: my part a Jewish mother with an idiot son whose weakness was to kill little girls and hide them in his mother's rag bag. My dialogue consisting of: "Oi, oi, oi; we shouldn't have left him alone." The producer thought I was little Stella. He couldn't believe I was 74. But *Who's Who* has it correctly, *Born 9th February 1865*. I hope to get away to the South of France to a little hotel at the same price but set in beauty—the lovely Ferme des Orangers with its nightingales, and the scent of the orange groves. . .
I am getting used to poverty and discomfort, and even to the very real unhappiness of having no one to give me an arm when I cross the road carrying "Moonbeam" through the terrifying tearing traffic. . . .

SHAW.
4 Whitehall Court,
21st August, 1939.
My dear Stella:

The giant is decrepit and his wife crippled with lumbago. . . . Yes, they wanted you for the part in the film but they gave up because you would not be separated for six months from your dog. For Heaven's sake, when that wretched little animal perishes in the course of nature or is slain by an automobile, buy a giant panda or a giraffe or a water buffalo or a sea lion, any of which you can take with you anywhere. They make affectionate pets, though the water buffalo has a dangerous preference for black children. Cheetahs are real dears: I have petted one. (*Turning away and withdrawing into himself.*) I am keeping away from Malvern this year; but my new play has enlivened the Festival. It is all about Charles II, his wife, two of his whores, an actress, Isaac Newton, his housekeeper and housemaid, Kneller the painter, George Fox, the first Quaker, and James II (Duke of York in the play). I have given up directing; (*Very slowly.*) I am too old, too old, too old. . . . (*He spaces out the final initials.*) G.B.S.

The LIGHTS have faded down for a moment around the two old artists, leaving a pinpoint on both of them. As they start to BLACK comes the final CURTAIN.

Also By

Jerome Kilty

DEAR LOVE

THE IDES OF MARCH

THE LITTLE BLACK BOOK (American version)

·   LOOK AWAY

Please visit our website **samuelfrench.com** for complete
descriptions and licensing information

THE CEMETERY CLUB
Ivan Menchell

Comedy / 1m, 5f / Multiple Sets

Three Jewish widows meet once a month for tea before going to visit their husband's graves. Ida is sweet tempered and ready to begin a new life, Lucille is a feisty embodiment of the girl who just wants to have fun, and Doris is priggish and judgmental, particularly when Sam the butcher enters the scene. He meets the widows while visiting his wife's grave. Doris and Lucille squash the budding romance between Sam and Ida. They are guilt stricken when this nearly breaks Ida's heart. The Broadway production starred Eileen Heckart as Lucille.

"Funny, sweet tempered, moving."
– *Boston Globe*

"Very touching and humorous. An evening of pure pleasure that will make you glad you went to the theatre."
– *Washington Journal Newspapers*

SAME TIME, NEXT YEAR
Bernard Slade

Comedy / 1m, 1f / Interior

One of the most popular romantic comedies of the century, *Same Time, Next Year* ran four years on Broadway, winning a Tony Award for lead actress Ellen Burstyn, who later recreated her role in the successful motion picture. It remains one of the world's most widely produced plays. The plot follows a love affair between two people, Doris and George, married to others, who rendezvous once a year. Twenty-five years of manners and morals are hilariously and touchingly played out by the lovers.

"Delicious wit, compassion, a sense of humor and a feel for nostalgia."
– *The New York Times*

"Genuinely funny and genuinely romantic."
– *The New York Post*

OTHER TITLES AVAILABLE FROM SAMUEL FRENCH

DEAR LOVE
Jerome Kilty

Biography / 1m, 1f

As the hit play *Dear Liar* drew on the life-long correspondence of Bernard Shaw and Mrs. Patrick Campbell, author Jerome Kilty uses the poems and letters of Elizabeth Barrett and Robert Browning to present this compelling portrait of a couple whose words and love are legendary. First corresponding via letters, Elizabeth thinks of Browning as merely "an acquaintance." Then his poetry moves her so deeply, they eventually meet. Chastised by her stern father and guilty over the death of her beloved brother, Elizabeth is bereft and isolated. Browning begins to court her and she is finally persuaded to marry and accompany him to Italy, where their love might grow away from the over-watchful eyes of her antagonistic, Victorian father. Elizabeth Barrett loved Robert Browning beyond all enduring; *Dear Love* recounts the ways.

SAMUEL FRENCH STAFF

Nate Collins
President

Ken Dingledine
Director of Operations,
Vice President

Bruce Lazarus
Executive Director

Rita Maté
Director of Finance

ACCOUNTING

Lori Thimsen | Director of Licensing Compliance
Nehal Kumar | Senior Accounting Associate
Josephine Messina | Accounts Payable
Helena Mezzina | Royalty Administration
Joe Garner | Royalty Administration
Jessica Zheng | Accounts Receivable
Andy Lian | Accounts Receivable
Zoe Qiu | Accounts Receivable
Charlie Sou | Accounting Associate
Joann Mannello | Orders Administrator

BUSINESS AFFAIRS

Lysna Marzani | Director of Business Affairs
Kathryn McCumber | Business Administrator

CUSTOMER SERVICE AND LICENSING

Brad Lohrenz | Director of Licensing Development
Billie Davis | Licensing Service Manager
Fred Schnitzer | Business Development Manager
Melody Fernandez | Amateur Licensing Supervisor
Laura Lindson | Professional Licensing Supervisor
John Tracey | Professional Licensing Associate
Kim Rogers | Amateur Licensing Associate
Matthew Akers | Amateur Licensing Associate
Jay Clark | Amateur Licensing Associate
Alicia Grey | Amateur Licensing Associate
Ashley Byrne | Amateur Licensing Associate
Jake Glickman | Amateur Licensing Associate
Chris Lonstrup | Amateur Licensing Associate
Jabez Zuniga | Amateur Licensing Associate
Glenn Halcomb | Amateur Licensing Associate
Derek Hassler | Amateur Licensing Associate
Jennifer Carter | Amateur Licensing Associate

EDITORIAL AND PUBLICATIONS

Amy Rose Marsh | Literary Manager
Ben Coleman | Editorial Associate
Gene Sweeney | Graphic Designer
David Geer | Publications Supervisor
Charlyn Brea | Publications Associate
Tyler Mullen | Publications Associate

MARKETING

Abbie Van Nostrand | Director of Marketing
Alison Sundstrom | Marketing Associate

OPERATIONS

Joe Ferreira | Product Development Manager
Casey McLain | Operations Supervisor
Danielle Heckman | Office Coordinator, Reception

SAMUEL FRENCH BOOKSHOP (LOS ANGELES)

Joyce Mehess | Bookstore Manager
Cory DeLair | Bookstore Buyer
Jennifer Palumbo | Customer Service Associate
Sonya Wallace | Bookstore Associate
Tim Coultas | Bookstore Associate
Monté Patterson | Bookstore Associate
Robin Hushbeck | Bookstore Associate
Alfred Contreras | Shipping & Receiving

LONDON OFFICE

Felicity Barks | Submissions Associate
Steve Blacker | Bookshop Associate
David Bray | Customer Services Associate
Zena Choi | Professional Licensing Associate
Robert Cooke | Assistant Buyer
Stephanie Dawson | Amateur Licensing Associate
Simon Ellison | Retail Sales Manager
Jason Felix | Royalty Administration
Susan Griffiths | Amateur Licensing Associate
Robert Hamilton | Amateur Licensing Associate
Lucy Hume | Publications Associate
Nasir Khan | Management Accountant
Simon Magniti | Royalty Administration
Louise Mappley | Amateur Licensing Associate
James Nicolau | Despatch Associate
Martin Phillips | Librarian
Zubayed Rahman | Despatch Associate
Steve sanderson | Royalty Administration Supervisor
Roger Sheppard | I.T. Manager
Geoffrey Skinner | Company Accountant
Peter Smith | Amateur Licensing Associate
Garry Spratley | Customer Service Manager
David Webster | UK Operations Director

GET THE NAME OF YOUR CAST AND CREW IN PRINT WITH SPECIAL EDITIONS!

Special Editions are a unique, fun way to commemorate your production and RAISE MONEY.

The Samuel French Special Edition is a customized script personalized to *your* production. Your cast and crew list, photos from your production and special thanks will all appear in a Samuel French Acting Edition alongside the original text of the play.

These Special Editions are powerful fundraising tools that can be sold in your lobby or throughout your community in advance.

These books have autograph pages that make them perfect for year book memories, or gifts for relatives unable to attend the show. Family and friends will cherish this one of a kind souvenier.

Everyone will want a copy of these beautiful, personalized scripts!

ORDER YOUR COPIES TODAY!
E-MAIL SPECIALEDITIONS@SAMUELFRENCH.COM
OR CALL US AT 1-866-598-8449!